TWO OLD
t toes
ME

ures by Carolyn Fisher

CHILDREN'S 21 day loan

PLACE IN RETURN BOX to remove this checkout from your record.
TO AVOID FINES return on or before date due.
MAY BE RECALLED with earlier due date if reqeusted.

DATE DUE	DATE DUE	DATE DUE
APR 0 2016	05 APR 2 8 2017	MetCat
MAY 0 2 2016		JUN 15 2017
0 5 0 3 1 0	JAN 0 8 2019	MAR 1 8 2019

11/13 20# purple K:/Proj/Acc&Pres/CIRC/DateDueForms_2013.indd - pg.10

D1446134

PZ
7
.C842455
T8
2013

For my dad, who taught me how to grow **potatoes**, and everything else.
-J.C.

Thanks to Norton Stillman for the idea.

For Stevie -C.F.

Text copyright © 2003, 2013 John Coy,
all rights reserved. Illustrations copyright
© 2003, 2013 Carolyn Fisher, all rights reserved.
No portion of this book may be reproduced in any
form without the written consent of Nodin Press.

ISBN: 978-1-935666-46-2
Previously published by Dragonfly Books
(ISBN: 978-0-440-41790-3)

Nodin Press
530 North 3rd Street
Suite 120
Minneapolis, MN,
55401

www.nodinpress.com

Last spring at my dad's house, I found

two old potatoes

in the back of the cupboard.

They were so OLD.

sprouts were growing

from their eyes.

"Grrrr."

I tossed them in the TRASH.

"Wait," DAD said. "I think we can grow new potatoes with those."

"I'll call your grandpa. He'll know."

After talking with Grandpa, Dad and I took the potatoes

Dad carefully cut the potatoes into nine pieces with his jackknife.

I made sure each piece had at least one yellow sprout.

Dad dug nine small holes. I put a piece of potato, with the eye facing up, in each hole.

Then I covered them with dirt to make little hills.

Dad got the hose

and I watered gently.

In May,

green plants poked up

like caterpillars unfolding.

We got down

on our knees

and picked weeds.

We shoveled compost onto each hill.

"Won't that smother the plants?"

"No. They'll grow through it."

"Are we really going to get new potatoes from old potatoes?"

"I think so," said Dad.

When we watered,
I accidentally sprayed my dad with the hose.

He laughed

and

sprayed me back.

IN JULY, when the plants were as tall as my waist, we picked potato beetles off the leaves.

"GROSS."

I dropped them into a pail of soapy water.

"We have
to do this,"
Dad said.

"otherwise, the bugs
will eat the leaves
and the potatoes won't grow."

In August,
some of the plants
turned brown and withered.

"Are they dead?"
"No," said Dad.

"The potatoes are
growing underground."

"Are you sure?"
"I hope so.
That's what your
grandpa said."

We weeded.

We Watered.

We Waited.

Now, on a cool September day, Dad and I sit on the bench in front of the garden.

"How's your bedroom at your mom's house coming?" Dad asks.

"Good. Mom and I painted it periwinkle."

"Periwinkle. I like that color. I bet it looks good."

"You can see it on Friday when you pick me up."

"Okay," Dad says. "It will be Periwinkle Friday."

We get up
and walk to the garden.
"What's your favorite way
to eat potatoes?" Dad asks.

"MASHED,
with lots of butter and
a sprinkle of nutmeg for good luck."

Dad gets the garden fork
from the shed
and I carry the big bucket.

Dad digs at the first hill.
Nothing but dirt.
He digs again. More dirt.

I dig deep. I lift the fork and see seven golden shapes. "Potatoes!" I shout.

"Look at those SPUDS," Dad says.

I bend down
pick up a potato
rub the dirt off its skin,
and set it in the bucket.

ONE potato, two potato, THREE Potato, four.

Five six potato, potato, potato, SEVEN POTATO, more

EACH HILL HaS LOtS oF PotAtOES.

SOME are SMaLL. SOME are BIG.

SOMe have FUNNY faces.

51 Potato, 52 Potato, 53 Potato, 54.

55 Potato, 56 Potato, 57 Potato,

more.

I count **Sixty-seven** and our bucket is **overflowing**.